Help me, Herman.

Herman the Helper

BY ROBERT KRAUS

PICTURES BY
JOSE ARUEGO & ARIANE DEWEY

Aladdin Paperbacks

Don't worry, I'll help you.

Aladdin Paperbacks
An imprint of Simon & Schuster
Children's Publishing Division
1230 Avenue of the Americas
New York, NY 10020

10   9   8

Originally published by Windmill Books, Inc.
Manufactured in the United States of America

Library of Congress Cataloging-in-Publication Data
Kraus, Robert, 1925-
    Herman the helper/by Robert Kraus; pictures by Jose Aruego & Ariane Dewey.
    p.   cm.
Reprint. Originally published: New York: Windmill Books, 1974.
Summary: Herman the helpful octopus is always willing to assist
anyone who needs his help—old or young, friend or enemy.
ISBN 0-671-66270-8 pbk
[1. Octopus—Fiction.   2. Brotherliness—Fiction.   3. Helpfulness—
Fiction.]   I. Aruego, Jose, ill.   II. Dewey, Ariane, ill.
III. Title.
[PZ7.K868HF 1987]   87-32071
[E]—dc19   CIP   AC

For Pamela, Bruce, Billy & Juan

Herman liked to help.

Thank you, Herman.

He helped his mother.

That's nice, Herman.

He helped his father.

That's my dad.

He helped his brothers and sisters.

Thank you, brother.

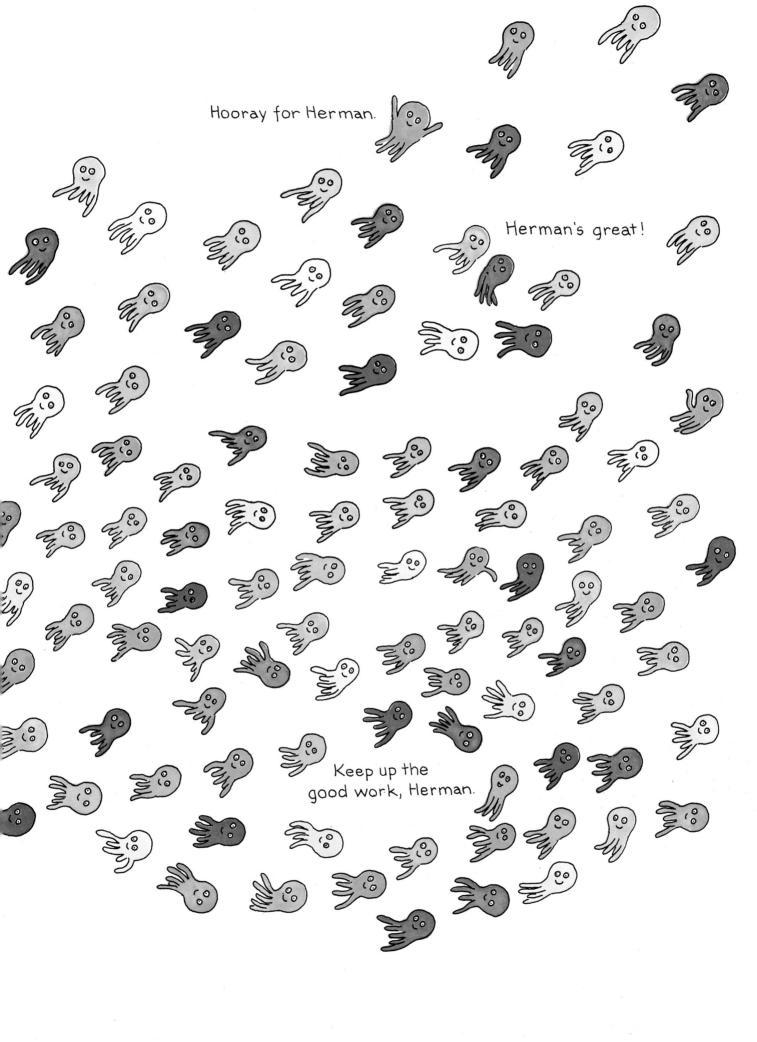

He helped his aunt.

What a beautiful bonnet, Herman.

Yes.

He helped his uncle.

He helped his friends.

Many thanks, Herman.

He helped his enemies.

Okay.

Help! It's after us!

I'll camouflage you with my ink.

Herman saved the day!

He helped the young.

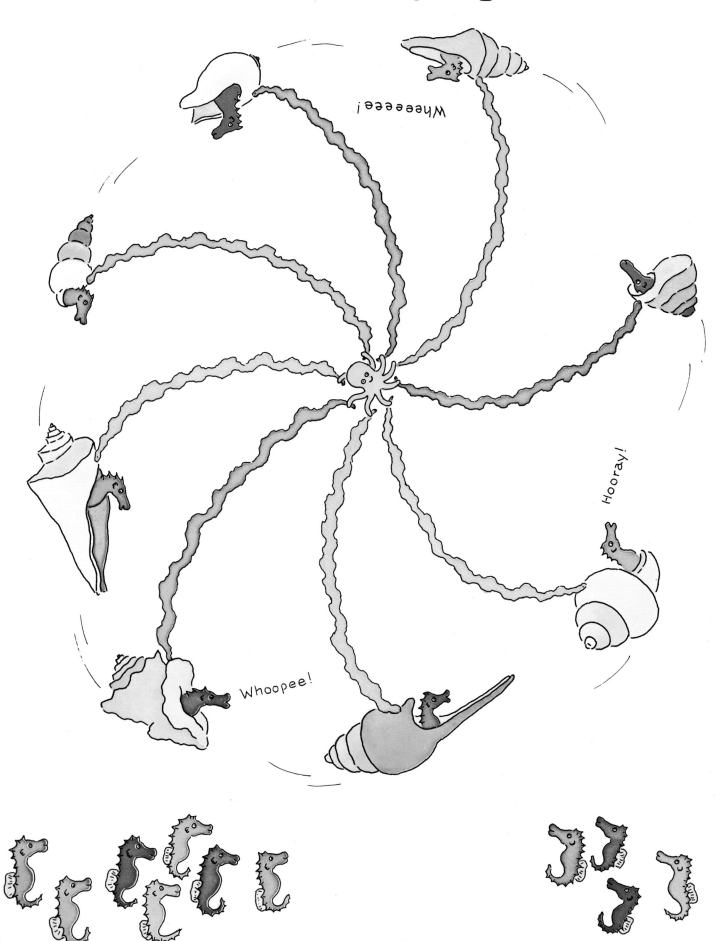

He helped the old.

Whoops!

This will help you swim.

He helped the poor and needy.

He helped the fireman.

Follow me.

He helped the policeman.

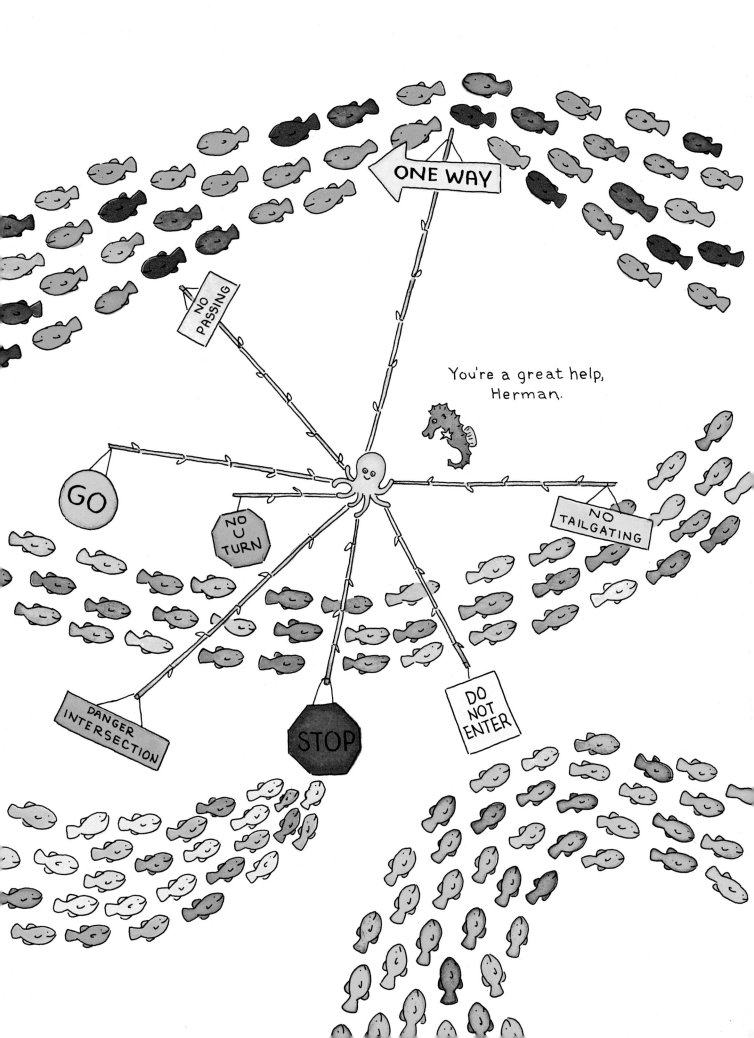

Then the clock struck six and Herman hurried home.

He washed his hands and face.

I'm hungry!

And sat down to supper.

"May I help you to some mashed potatoes?" asked Herman's father.

"No thanks,"
said Herman,
"I'll help myself."

Thank you,
Herman.